Bank Street

ABOUT THE BANK STREET READY-TO-READ SERIES

More than seventy-five years of educational research, innovative teaching, and quality publishing have earned The Bank Street College of Education its reputation as America's most trusted name in early childhood education.

Because no two children are exactly alike in their development, the Bank Street Ready-to-Read series is written on three levels to accommodate the individual stages of reading readiness of children ages three through eight.

○ *Level 1:* GETTING READY TO READ (Pre-K–Grade 1)
Level 1 books are perfect for reading aloud with children who are getting ready to read or just starting to read words or phrases. These books feature large type, repetition, and simple sentences.

● *Level 2:* READING TOGETHER (Grades 1–3)
These books have slightly smaller type and longer sentences. They are ideal for children beginning to read by themselves who may need help.

○ *Level 3:* I CAN READ IT MYSELF (Grades 2–3)
These stories are just right for children who can read independently. They offer more complex and challenging stories and sentences.

All three levels of The Bank Street Ready-to-Read books make it easy to select the books most appropriate for your child's development and enable him or her to grow with the series step by step. The levels purposely overlap to reinforce skills and further encourage reading.

We feel that making reading fun is the single most important thing anyone can do to help children become good readers. We hope you will become part of Bank Street's long tradition of learning through sharing.

The Bank Street College of Education

To Debbie
—M.S.

THE PLANT THAT KEPT ON GROWING

A Bantam Book/July 1996

*Published by Bantam Doubleday Dell Books
for Young Readers, a division of Bantam
Doubleday Dell Publishing Group, Inc.
1540 Broadway, New York, New York 10036.*

Series graphic design by Alex Jay/Studio J

Special thanks to Irmeli Holmberg, Hope Innelli and Kathy Huck.

Library of Congress Cataloging-in-Publication Data

Brenner, Barbara.
*The plant that kept on growing / by Barbara Brenner :
illustrated by Melissa Sweet.
p.   cm. — (Bank Street ready-to-read)
"A Byron Preiss book."
Summary: After Will and his sister plant
lots of seeds in hopes of winning a prize
at the 4-H fair, they are surprised
to see the appearance of a giant
tomato plant that will not stop growing.
ISBN 0-553-37578-4
[1. Plants—Fiction.   2. Fairs—Fiction.   3. Stories in rhyme.]
I. Sweet, Melissa, ill.   II. Title.   III. Series.
PZ8.3.B747Pl   1996
[E]—dc20
95-18798   CIP   AC*

Published simultaneously in the United States and Canada

PRINTED IN THE UNITED STATES OF AMERICA

0 9 8 7 6 5 4 3 2 1

Bank Street Ready-to-Read™

The Plant That Kept On Growing

by Barbara Brenner
Illustrated by Melissa Sweet

A Byron Preiss Book

BANTAM BOOKS
NEW YORK • TORONTO • LONDON • SYDNEY • AUCKLAND

This is the story
of Will and me
and the time we grew
the amazing tree.

4

It happened the year
we had our eyes
on winning the 4-H
garden prize.

My twin and I
were set to grow
the very best plant
in the 4-H show.

So when May came
we picked a spot.
We dug ourselves
a garden plot.

Will planted squash,
bush peas, and beans.
I planted melons
and mustard greens.

And as we dropped
the last seed in,
we said, "With a little
luck we'll win."

9

First came the rain.
Then came the sun.
Our seeds all sprouted
—every one.

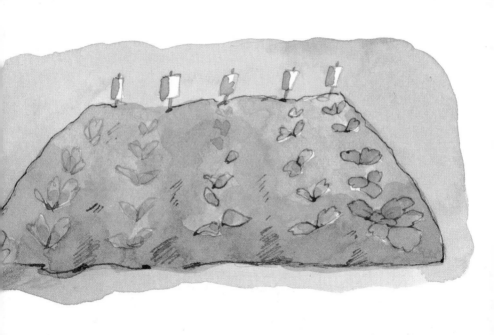

But as our plants
began to grow,
they vanished—row
by row by row!

11

First a woodchuck
stole Will's peas
without so much as
asking "Please."

Worms ate the squash.

Bugs got the beans.

Rabbits ate the melons
and mustard greens.

13

Soon Will and I
felt sick with doubt.
We thought our luck
was running out.

But wait! Our plot
was not all bare!
One green plant
was growing there!

It poked right up
from a small dirt hill.
"I wonder what that is,"
said Will.

Whatever it was,
that plant was growing.
And it kept going—
going—GOING!

It grew six feet
in half an hour.
It sent out branches . . .
leaves . . . a flower!

Then came a small fruit,
round and green.
It looked like nothing
we'd ever seen.

The fruit turned yellow!
Then orange! Then red!
Soon it grew bigger
than Willy's head!

Now Will and I
could plainly see—
That plant was—
A GIANT TOMATO TREE!

And how it grew!
By Monday noon
that tomato looked
like a weather balloon.

By the following
Friday night
it was almost the size
of a satellite!

The next day was
the 4-H fair.
How could we get
that tomato there?

24

It wouldn't fit
in any truck.
It looked as if
we might be stuck.

But brother Will
stirred up a fuss
and got the fair
to come to us!

Folks could not
believe their eyes
when they saw our
tomato surprise.

Of course we won
the big Grand Prize!

Next day we took
our tomato down.
We shared it with
the entire town.

28

We sliced it up
with a power saw.
We cooked up some.
We ate some raw.

29

Tomato salad!
Tomato soup!
Tomato sauce
for a hungry group!

And we made the last
of our juicy prize

into two hundred
yummy pizza pies!